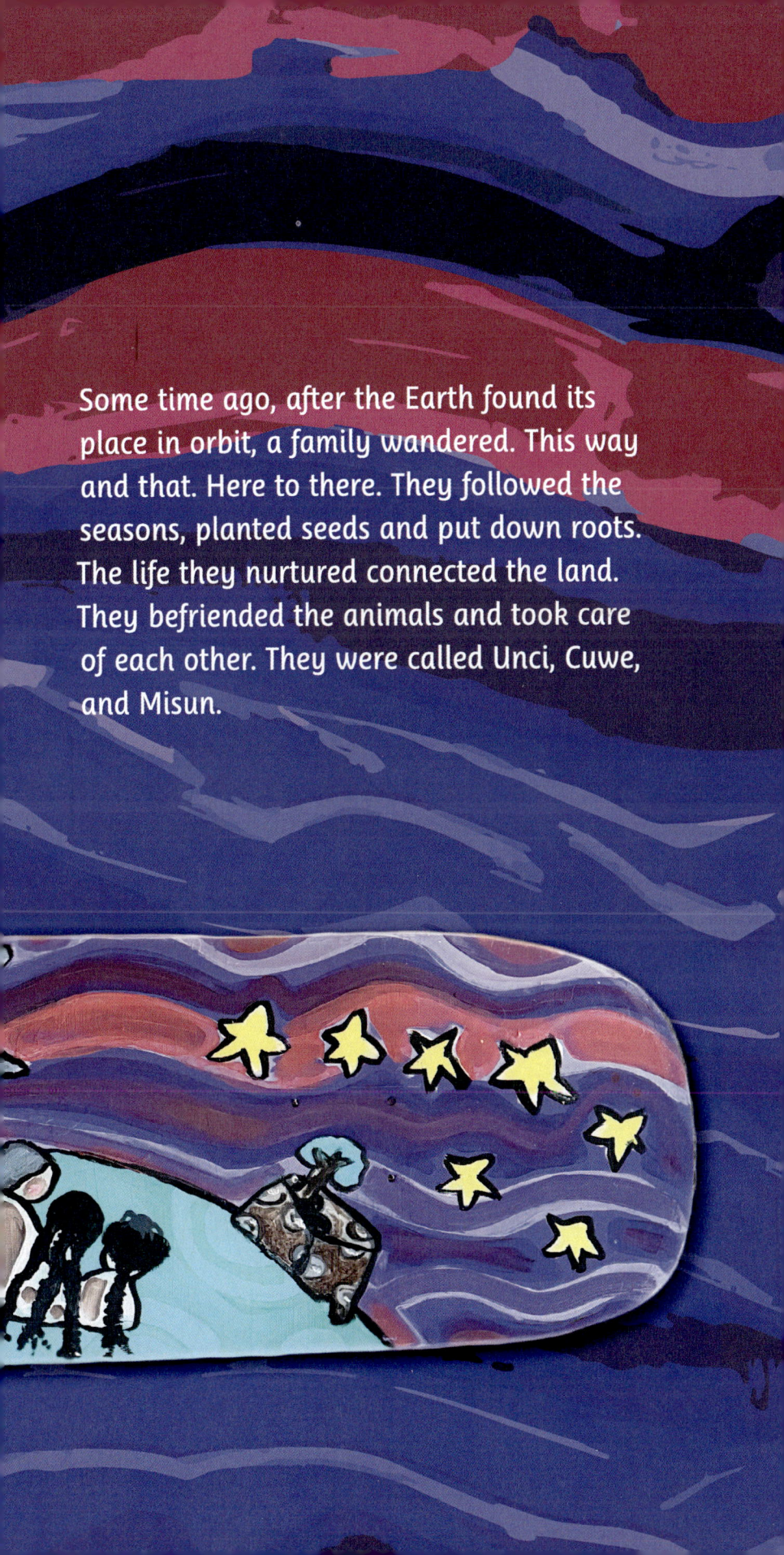

Some time ago, after the Earth found its place in orbit, a family wandered. This way and that. Here to there. They followed the seasons, planted seeds and put down roots. The life they nurtured connected the land. They befriended the animals and took care of each other. They were called Unci, Cuwe, and Misun.

Unci took care of everyone. She was the grandmother of Cuwe and Misun. As she planted seeds, she taught the children the Star Knowledge. The stars after all are where we all came from, and one day we will be called back.

Cuwe took her role as oldest child very seriously.

She listened intently to the lessons and stories Unci told, especially the ones about her mother, who had left the earth before Cuwe could remember her. Cuwe was never short on questions. The "whys" and "hows" where usually followed by "whens" and "wheres".

She always wanted to make her grandmother, mother, and herself proud. She wanted to be the best big sister. Sometimes that meant having a lot of patience.

Misun was the youngest. He wanted to be the best Misun. He could talk to every animal. They were all his friends. However, his best friend was a spider called Iktomi. Oh boy! They were naughty. Their favorite game was playing tricks on Cuwe.

One night, while Unci brushed Cuwe's hair, she told her about the timpsula, a wild turnip that grew strong roots underground. All the "hows" and "why" we plant it. How it connects us to creation and strengthens the Earth. While Unci braided Cuwe's hair, she talked about her mother. Cuwe loved hearing these stories. Unci pointed to the sky and called Cuwe's mother her fallen star. She explained how she had used a timpsula braid to connect to love.

Their mother had fallen in love with Wicahpi, a great spirit who lived in the star world. Their mother found the highest point of earth and used the timpsula

braid to climb and connect with the children's father. However, one night she was overwhelmed with love and became distracted, causing her to fall, leaving the children orphaned.

"We will all make our journey when the stars call us back," said Unci.

"How will I know where to go?" Cuwe asked nervously.

Unci placed a hand on Cuwe's shoulder and softly said, "You will find your way."

Cuwe worried. What if she couldn't?

The very next morning Unci was gone.
Her spirit decided it was time to walk
on with the ancestors. She left behind
all her possessions, the children, and her
earthly body.

Her journey began while the moon was the
highest and the stars were the brightest.
Cuwe felt sad. She wanted to make her
grandmother, her mother, and herself proud.
She wanted to be the best big sister.

While gathering and bundling Unci's things,
Cuwe decided to keep just one very
special item. Unci's abalone
shell. She burned sage, sweet
grass and said a prayer.
She hoped Unci found
her way.

Misun watched as Cuwe brought the stones from the fire into the inipi, the sweat lodge she built to honor Unci. He felt small. He wanted his grandmother, his mother, and Cuwe to be proud of him. He wanted to be the best Misun. He needed something to help Cuwe feel brave. He wanted himself to feel powerful. He wanted to remind them both of Unci's wisdom.

He knew exactly what to do. He asked his animal friends for advice.

Misun found the perfect creature to help them feel powerful, to give them courage and remind them of their grandmother's wisdom.

Or so he thought.

As Cuwe stepped out of the inipi she heard a loud screech. There was the biggest owl she had ever seen perched right on top. Cuwe was terrified. She turned to run.

When she did, she tripped, and Unci's abalone shell flew out of her hands. As it landed it cracked in half. The only thing Cuwe had left of Unci was gone. Cuwe felt broken.

She got to her feet and ran. She needed her mother and Unci. She thought this was just another one of Misuns' tricks and was angry with him. She didn't want to be a big sister.

Cuwe ran towards the highest point she could find. She climbed all the way to the top. She wanted to touch the stars. She wanted Unci and her mother. She sat there and cried. She cried and cried until her tears created an ocean around her. The only land that remained was the island of grief that surrounded her. That's where she stayed.

She stayed so long her braids connected to the ground and began to take root. Cuwe was ready to give up. She closed her eyes and took a deep breath. She thought of Unci and her stories about why we plant the seeds that connect us to creation, strengthen our roots, and to take care of each other.

"How will I do this without you?" whispered Cuwe.

Cuwe looked to the stars and heard her grandmother's voice coming from within her heart.

"You will find your way." said the voice.

Cuwe felt comfort. She wanted to make Unci, her mother, and herself proud. She wanted to be the best big sister. She reached up with all her energy and pulled herself out of the ground. Cuwe felt strong. The force of her strength made the Earth rumble and shake. Out of the ocean a very large and very old turtle rose under her feet. Cuwe felt ready. Together they set out to find Misun.

When the flood happened, Misun and his animal friends had to cling to the last bits of remaining earth. He was doing all he could to hang on. His feet were slowly sliding into the endless waves caused by Cuwe's mourning.

All his friends were helping. The spider, Iktomi, spun a sticky web that kept him secured to the rocks. The muskrat dove deep for soil to keep the rocks steady. The fish kept him company while the crow flew high above the waves searching for any sign of Cuwe.

Everyone was growing more and more exhausted. Misun felt alone. He should have been a better brother and listened less to Iktomi. He needed his sister.

Just as the web was starting to break free from the rock and the muskrat hadn't returned from the depths, Misun started to give up. The fish had swum away, and the crow couldn't see over a tremendous wave that was coming straight for Misun and Iktomi. They were scared. Just as they were almost swept off the rock, and all hope was lost, the giant turtle broke through the water. Cuwe was on its back.

She climbed down as fast as she could, using a timpsula braid, and snatched her brother up to safety. Misun was grateful. Cuwe felt proud.

She felt like a great big sister.

As Cuwe and Misun comforted each other, the sea around them began to calm. They floated on the back of the turtle and spoke of the future. Together they would set out to plant the seeds that connected them to all of creation.

This time, Misun was the one with all the questions.

"How will we know where to go?" he asked.

Cuwe touched his shoulder gently and said, "Misunkala, we will find our way".

# Glossary

**Abalone Shell** — A mollusk shell, generally obtained through trading, that has become used to burn herbs in ceremonies.

**Cuwe** — Big sister.

**Iktomi** — In Lakota stories, Iktomi is a spider-trickster spirit, shapeshifter, and often a socially inappropriate role model.

**Inipi** — Sweat lodge.

**Misun** — Little brother.

**Misunkala** — A term of endearment for little brother.

**Timpsula** — Wild turnip.

**Unci** — Grandmother.

**Wicahpi** — Star. Wicahpi Owanjila is known as the North Star. He is believed to stay in one place caused by a broken heart after losing his wife.

## About the Author

My story began in Los Angeles County, California where I was born and raised. I am the middle child of six kids. My parents came from severe trauma and weren't equipped with the coping skills or support needed to break the cycle, so unfortunately passed the trauma down to us. I wouldn't say my childhood was a happy one, however, some of the more positive memories I have are of my paternal grandmother and big sister.

My grandmother was our family's matriarch, and her house was a safe stable space for the kids. We would often sit and listen as she recalled her childhood. She was a pious woman. All her stories had underlying lessons, taught values, and directed us to always do the right thing, ultimately, teaching us to be good people. I loved to imagine what life was like for her and have those glimpses of where she came from. My big sister, my Cuwe, always seemed older than what she was. I imagine it was because of the responsibility of being the eldest and enduring her own personal experiences. She got all the kids ready for school and looked after us when my parents didn't have the capacity. She was the one to drive miles to show up for me in my early adult years, and even when she didn't want to be, she was my mother figure. I will be forever grateful to her. The common factor in each woman was that no matter the trials and tribulations they personally encountered, their hearts were always filled with care for me.

When I started middle school, my mother wanting to be closer to our Native American heritage, moved us from Los Angeles to Lakota Homes Indian Housing in Rapid City, S.D. Without previous immersion, we dove headfirst into being Oglala Lakota. This new exciting culture opened to me. Although I often felt like I didn't fit in, the family and peers I met, warmly welcomed us. Even though we were from different places we still had something that connected us.

Unfortunately, family life rapidly deteriorated and we became a broken home. After a couple of years, it was time for me to start healing. I began the emancipation process and moved to Illinois to finish high school. I was without my birth family, in an entirely new state and trying to figure out my identity. I was lost. Luckily, I found the skateboarding and punk rock community. They saved me. Even if I wasn't the best skater and I didn't know how to play music, it was a place I could seek out wherever it existed, and I could be accepted. I could still push around, make art, or sing along to the music. It didn't matter where I came from. I was home.

I believe we all have an Unci, Cuwe, Misun, and Iktomi in our personal stories. We possess the knowledge of the past, the need to protect, and the desire to uplift the younger generation and the courage to fulfill our roles. Sometimes we are misguided and sometimes we are the troublemakers. Together we make each other complete. Essentially, this story brings familiar tales, told by our elders, with the goal of reigniting their imaginations and opening dialogue to revive the younger generations. These stories are the basis of who we are and together we can give them new life. The characters reach children at their level and uplift them. It's important to look deep within our selves to draw out strength to persevere. It's about connecting to our roots, realizing you are enough, and working together towards a positive future.

## Why Use Skateboards?

Skateboarding has a prominent role in my life. It has also become an important tool in connecting to a platform that serves the Native community. I grew up around skating and it was a critical asset while learning who I was as an individual. Furthermore, while visiting my sister on the Cheyenne River Reservation, in Eagle Butte, South Dakota, I witnessed children eager to skate, but they were without access to skateboards. This was a community that has generationally struggled with drug and alcohol abuse, poverty, and a severely high youth suicide rate. I was reminded of where I came from and wanted to help. I've experienced what skateboarding can do for an individual and have seen how the skate community brings people together, connects, and empowers them.

 My sister and I began organizing resources and doing what we could to fill the skate needs of the youth. I wanted them to know the love and security skateboarding provides, so like me, they could also find hope. When I began this project, I knew I wanted to use recycled skateboards. Like my stories, I wanted to breathe new life into the decks and give them a second chance at reaching whoever needed them. I firsthand know that skateboarding can save lives and I hoped that my stories could, at the very least, touch some lives as well.

 My mission is to help kids like myself find their way in this world as I try to be the adult that I needed growing up to my own children. It's about a need. We need to look at the teachings that exist and apply them to what is relevant now. We need to tell our stories so that they can reach our youth that otherwise feel like they have no voice. I would like to use funding I raise by this book, and future endeavors, to put into skate, art, and literary programs on the reservation. It's important to provide a platform for other young people to tell their own stories. Our roots connect us, skateboarding connects us, storytelling passes down our knowledge and bridges the gap where we could feel a disconnect. If we keep pushing on, we will find our way and together we can write a positive future.

# We Will Find Our Way

© 2022 by Cynthia Harding

All rights reserved. No reproduction in any form whatsoever except with the written permission of the publisher.

ISBN 979-8-9862981-2-2

Book cover and interior design by Paul Nylander | Illustrada

## Black Bears & Blueberries Publishing

www.blackbearsandblueberries.com

A Native owned non-profit publishing company, with a focus on creating and developing Native children's books for all young people written by Native authors and illustrators.